Goldilocks and the Three Bears
❧ Fairy Tale Treasury ❧

Adapted by
Jane Jerrard

Illustrations by
Burgandy Nilles

Publications International, Ltd.

There once was a family of three bears—a great big Papa Bear, a middle-size Mama Bear, and a wee little Baby Bear.

The bears lived in a neat little house right in the middle of a forest. Every day started just the same way. They sat down and had a breakfast of hot porridge.

One sunny summer morning, Mama Bear spooned the porridge into their three bowls. "It's too hot!" squeaked Baby Bear, tasting the porridge in his wee little bowl.

"Ouch! We need to let it cool off," growled Papa Bear, after he tried the porridge in his big bowl.

So the three bears decided to go for a walk while their hot breakfast cooled.

Meanwhile, a little girl named Goldilocks was out walking in the woods that day, all by herself.

She was feeling rather hungry, though she had eaten her own breakfast earlier. When she saw the bears' house, she thought it was just the place to find a bite to eat. She marched right up to the door and knocked, but there was no answer.

So Goldilocks just let herself in!

Goldilocks saw the three bowls of porridge and decided she simply must have some. First, she took a taste from the great big bowl. "Oooh, this is too hot!" she cried.

Next, she tried the middle-size bowl. "This one's too cold!" she said.

Then she had a taste from the wee little bowl. "This is just right!" she said, and she gobbled it all up.

After she had eaten, Goldilocks wanted to rest. She saw three chairs and sat down first in the great big chair. "This is too hard!" she said.

Next, she tried the middle-size chair. "This is too soft!" said Goldilocks, struggling to get out.

Then Goldilocks tried the wee little chair. "This is just right!" she exclaimed. But she sat down so hard the chair broke all to pieces.

By this time, Goldilocks was very tired. She went upstairs and found three beds. First, she tried the great big bed. "This one's too high at the head!"

Next, she tried the middle-size bed. "This one's too high at the foot!" she cried in disgust.

Last, she lay down on the wee little bed. Sure enough, she said, "This one's just right!" And she fell fast asleep.

When the three bears returned home from their walk, they noticed that things were not quite right.

Papa Bear said in his great big voice, "Someone's been eating my porridge!" Then Mama Bear said in her middle-size voice, "Someone's been eating my porridge."

Baby Bear said in his wee little voice, "Someone's been eating my porridge—AND HAS EATEN IT ALL UP!"

When he saw his big, hard chair, Papa Bear said in his great big voice, "Someone's been sitting in my chair!"

"Someone's been sitting in my chair!" said Mama Bear in her middle-size voice.

Baby Bear squeaked in his wee little voice, "Someone's been sitting in my chair—AND HAS BROKEN IT ALL UP!"

Next, the bears tiptoed upstairs.

"Someone's been sleeping in my bed!" said Papa Bear in his great big voice.

"Someone's been sleeping in my bed!" said Mama Bear in her middle-size voice. And Baby Bear cried, "Someone's been sleeping in my bed—AND SHE'S STILL IN IT!"

At this, Goldilocks awoke, jumped out the window and ran off as fast as she could. And the three bears never saw Goldilocks again.